GRANNY REARDUN

Joseph watched as the Allmans' house was pulled down. It had been built of good dimension stone, and there was no more left in the quarry. That's why the Allmans had to go. Joseph did not want to believe that a house could be pulled down just to make more stone.

There was already too much of it: his grandfather was a stonemason, and the village was full of his work. Joseph knew that he would have to do something else if he was to make his own life. He had to be different from his grandfather, and stone felt heavy and cruel.

This is the story of the day Joseph decided his future: many years later his story comes to an end in *Tom Fobble's Day*, just as his grandfather's story began in *The Stone Book*.

GRANNY REARDUN

ALAN GARNER

Etchings by Michael Foreman

COLLINS
St James's Place London

William Collins Sons & Co Ltd
London · Glasgow · Sydney · Auckland
Toronto · Johannesburg

First published 1977
© Alan Garner 1977
© Illustrations Michael Foreman 1977

ISBN 0 00 184288 9

Phototypeset by Tradespools Ltd, Frome, Somerset
Made and Printed in Great Britain by
W & J Mackay Limited, Chatham
by Photo-litho

for Elizabeth

GRANNY REARDUN

They were flitting the Allmans. Joseph sat
at the top of Leah's Bank and watched.

The horse and cart stood outside the
house, by the field gate. Elijah Allman
lifted the dollytub onto the cart first and set
it in the middle. Then Alice and Amelia
climbed into the dollytub, and Elijah
packed them round with bedding. Young
Herbert was carrying chairs.

The Allmans loaded the cart with furniture, stacking from the girls in the dolly-tub, so that the load was firm. Mrs Allman came out of the house backwards on her knees. She was donkey-stoning the doorstep white, and when she had done she stood up, and reached over the step and pulled the door to.

Elijah helped her up onto the carter's seat. Young Herbert sat next to her, holding the reins. Elijah took the bridle and walked the horse through the field gateway, down the Hough and onto the Moss.

Joseph listened to them go. He went to the top corner post of the field, ran three strides and slid down Leah's Bank. It was such a steep hill, and the grass so hard and slippery, that he could slide for yards at a time, standing. And when the grass was brogged by old cow muck, he had only to keep his balance, skip, and be away again.

He pushed the door open.

The house smelt wet with donkey-stone and limewash. The rooms were enormous

empty. All the floors were white, all the walls and beams and the ceilings white. The stairs were sand-scoured, and the boards too. There was no dirt anywhere.

Joseph looked out of the bedroom window. The Allmans were away across the Moss. He left the house and went home for breakfast. He lived at the bottom of the hill.

Grandfather had finished his breakfast and was smoking a pipe of tobacco in his chair by the fire. His hard fingers could press the tobacco down hot in the bowl, without burning himself.

"They've flitted Allmans," said Joseph.

"Ay," said Grandfather.

"What for?" said Joseph.

"The years they've been there," said Grandfather. "It's a wonderful thing, them in their grandeur, and us in raddle and daub."

"Why?" said Joseph.

"Eat your pobs," said Grandmother.

Grandfather knocked the ashes of his pipe

out onto his hand and pitched them in the fire. He raised himself. "Best be doing," he said. "Damper Latham's getting for me. And think on," he said to Joseph, "I'll have half an hour from you before school. Is your mother coming up for her dinner today?"

"And fetching Charlie," said Joseph. "She promised."

Grandfather picked up his canvas bass and took his cap off the doornail. The chisels and hammers clinked together in the bass. "Be sharp," he said to Joseph.

Grandfather was old. But he still turned out. He was building a wall into the hedge bank of Long Croft field, down the road from the house, under the wood.

Joseph washed his basin and spoon at the spring in the garden, and ran down the road to Long Croft.

Grandfather was rough-dressing the stone for the wall, and laying it out along the hedge. Joseph unwound the line and pegged one end in the joints where Grandfather had finished the day before, and pulled the line tight against the bank. His job was to cut the bank back to receive the stone and to run a straight bed for the bottom course.

He chopped at the bank.

"Sweep up behind you," said Grandfather. "Muck's no use on the road. It wants to be on the field."

Joseph had to throw the clods high over his head to clear the quickthorn hedge.

"Get your knee aback of your shovel," said Grandfather. "There's no sense in mauling yourself half to death. Come on, youth. Shape!"

Joseph chopped, shovelled and threw. Grandfather worked the stone.

"I don't know why I bother," he said. "I'd as lief let it lie. The rubbish they send! I doubt there's not above a hundred years in it. Watch your line!"

Joseph was sweating. Grandfather took the spade from him and looked along the bank. He walked down the raw cut edge and shaved the earth with light swings of the blade. "You've got it like a fiddler's elbow," he said.

Damper Latham came with his cart up the road under the wood from Chorley. The cart was heavy and pulled by two Shires. Their brasses glinted. Suns, moons and clovers chimed on their leathers. Damper Latham kept his horses smart as a show.

"Now then, Robert," he said.

Grandfather looked over the side of the cart. "What's all this?" he said. "It's never stone."

Damper Latham winked at Joseph. "Eh, dear, dear! Robert?" he said. "Has the Missis been sitting on your shirt tail?"

"Take it away," said Grandfather. "I'll not put me name to it."

Damper Latham let down the boards and the sides of the cart and climbed onto the load. He began to walk the stones to the edge and slide them down two planks to Grandfather.

"You'll take what you're given, Robert," he said. "Else go without. I've had a job for to get these."

Grandfather grunted, and swung the blocks to lie as he wanted. They seemed to move without more than his hand on them.

Joseph tried to help, but he couldn't even pull the weight from the slope of the plank. He pulled and shoved, and the block shifted its balance and came at him. He couldn't stop it and he couldn't put it down and it was fighting him. He twisted away, but he still couldn't let go. The living dead weight of it all gripped his hands and wrenched his shoulders. Then it fell clear and smashed on the road.

"You great nowt!" shouted Grandfather. "See at what you've done!"

Joseph ran up the plank to the cart.

"See at it!" shouted Grandfather. "I can't use that! I'm not a man with string round his britches!"

The chapel clock struck eight.

"There's not better to be got, Robert," said Damper Latham.

"Well, I'll not abide it," said Grandfather.

"Must I go fetch you a load from Leah's

14

Bank?" said Damper Latham.

"No!"

"Where's stone on Leah's Bank?" said Joseph.

"It's eight o'clock," said Grandfather. "Time you were off."

"Stay and give us a tune," said Damper Latham. "I'm going down the village. You can have a ride."

"He'll be late," said Grandfather.

"He'll not," said Damper Latham. "The E-Flat's under me coat there."

Joseph picked up the bright cornet from beneath the seat and set his tongue to the mouthpiece and loosened the valves with his fingers.

"What must I play?" he said.

"Give us a Methody hymn for to fetch this load off," said Damper Latham. "One with a swing."

Joseph played "Man Frail and God Eternal" twice. Grandfather and Damper Latham worked together, as they had always done. The stone moved lightly for them.

"*The busy tribes of flesh and blood, with all their lives and cares,*" sang Damper Latham, "*are carried downwards by the flood, and lost in following years.*"

"Couldn't wait," said Grandfather. "One week to flit. Out."

"Where've they gone?" said Damper Latham.

"The Moss," said Grandfather.

"Give us a swing, youth!" Damper Latham nudged Joseph. Joseph had stopped playing.

"Let's have some Temperance," said Grandfather.

So Joseph played "Dip your Roll in your own Pot at Home".

"How's Elijah?" said Damper Latham.

"Badly," said Grandfather. "Them as can't bend, like as not they break."

"Eh," said Damper Latham, and he looked both ways on the road before he spoke. "Is it true what it's for? A kitchen garden?"

"True? It's true!" said Grandfather. "Kitchen garden! Rector's wife must grow herself a vine and a twothree figs, seemingly. She caught a dose of religion, that one; and there's Allmans out. Hey!"

Joseph was looking at his own stretched face in the swell of the cornet. Someone must have taken the brass and shaped it and turned it, with valves for every note, tapping, drawing it to soprano E-Flat.

"Hey! Let's hear 'Ode to Drink'. This lot wants some raunging." The cart shook as Grandfather pulled at the base of the stack.

Joseph sucked for spit, but his mouth had dried.

Grandfather and Damper Latham began without him, and he had to catch up when his lips were wet.

"Let thy devotee extol thee,
And thy wondrous virtues sum;
But the worst of names I'll call thee,
O thou hydra monster Rum!"

The stones thumped off.

17

> *"Pimple-maker, visage-bloater,*
>   *Health-corrupter, idler's mate;*
> *Mischief-breeder, vice-promoter,*
>   *Credit-spoiler, devil's bait!"*

Damper Latham swept the cart with his broom, and danced and marched to Joseph's music. Grandfather had his chisels out and was hitting the notes on them with his hammer, like a xylophone.

> *"Utterance-boggler, stench-emitter,*
>   *Strong-man sprawler, fatal drop;*
> *Tumult-raiser, venom-spitter,*
>   *Wrap-inspirer, coward's prop!"*

Joseph had stopped playing. His neck hurt for thought of the Allmans. He couldn't swallow. But Grandfather and Damper Latham went on, singing louder and louder, tenor and bass, by turns.

Joseph shut his eyes.

> *"Virtue-blaster, base deceiver!*
>   *Spite-displayer, sot's delight!*
> *Noise-exciter, stomach-heaver!*
>   *Falsehood-spreader! Scorpion's bite!"*

18

Grandfather and Damper Latham were laughing too much to work.

Joseph opened his eyes. He was looking straight into Grandfather's, and they were hard, fierce, kind and blue.

"That's it, youth," said Grandfather. "Skrike or laugh. You'll learn."

Damper Latham backed the cart round for the village. "Shall you be wanting anything, Robert?" he said.

"If you're going by the smithy, tell Jump I need a four-pounder. And tell him I'll see him."

"Right you are, Robert," said Damper Latham. "Coom-agen, coom-agen," he called to the horses, and the two Shires scraped sparks with their shoes, and pulled. Damper Latham nodded towards the brass cornet in Joseph's hands and went on singing, his head and shoulders going back and to like a big clock.

"Quarrel-plotter, rage-discharger,
Giant-conqueror, wasteful sway . . ."

Joseph picked up the tune again.

"Chin-carbuncler, tongue-enlarger!
Malice-venter, Death's broad way!"

Grandfather was singing, too, and striking the chisels. His voice and their ringing faded. Joseph played and played.

"Tempest-scatterer, window-smasher,
Death-forerunner, hell's dire brink!
Ravenous murderer, windpipe-slasher,
Drunkard's lodging, meat and drink!"

Damper Latham and Joseph rode in silence. After the music, the horses and the cart were a quietness.

"Your Grandfather: he was a bit upset, that's all," said Damper Latham. "It's hard, at his time of day."

"I know," said Joseph.

"After all the tremendous work he's done. And now I can't hardly get him enough red rubbish for a length of wall – him as has cut only the best dimension stone all these years. It comes very hard."

"He wants me to follow him," said

Joseph.

Damper Latham looked sideways quickly.

"And shall you?"

"No."

"What shall you do, then? Go for a brick-setter?"

"No. I don't know."

"When do you finish your schooling?"

"Today," said Joseph.

"And you're not prenticed?"

"Me Grandfather thinks I'll be with him. But I'll never," said Joseph.

"I've been getting for Robert thirty years," said Damper Latham. "And there isn't the call on it now. Everywhere's brick. They want setters, not getters."

Joseph looked at the brass cornet. "Is it correct about Allmans?"

"Ay."

"They've been put out?"

"Ay."

"For a garden wall?"

"Ay."

"What's wrong with bricks for a garden?" said Joseph.

"Wouldn't suit," said Damper Latham. "And that house is the last dimension in the Hough. They had to flit."

The Shires stopped without telling when they came to the smithy. Damper Latham hitched their reins and went into the farrier's yard and down the wide steps to the cellar where the forge stood. Joseph put the cornet back under the seat and followed, quietly.

The smith and all his gang were working in a red and black light, hammermen every one of them, and making things. The noise was tremendous.

"Now then, Jump!" shouted Damper Latham.

"Now then, Damper!" shouted the smith, and all the hammering and the noise stopped. Horseshoes quenched in the trough.

Joseph stayed back from the men, watching, near the bellows of the forge. The long handle of the bellows was above him in the shadow.

The gang sat down and drew their beer from a keg under the bench and gave Damper Latham his mug.

Joseph reached up and put his fingers round the bellows handle. The ashwood was like silk to touch. He gripped hold to feel, and the handle moved before he could stop it. It moved just once, down and up, and the bellows breathed, and the coals glowed.

The smith looked, and saw Joseph. Joseph kept hold of the handle.

"That'll do, youth," said the smith gently, but he meant it.

Joseph let go.

"Best be off," said Damper Latham.

Joseph turned away from the warmth and the busy men together, up the steps into the farrier's yard and daylight, and he went excited.

The chapel clock struck nine.

Joseph was late for school. He could hear

its bell ringing the scholars in. He looked up at the chapel spire. At opposite ends of the village stood the two great pieces of Grandfather's life: church and chapel. They marked the village for him. Saint Philip's had a bigger steeple, and the chapel had the clock.

Joseph walked down the village towards the school and Saint Philip's, over the station bridge. Everything he saw was clear. He knew something he didn't know. It was the bell. It was the clock. It was the spires!

Grandfather had worked the chapel, but he had not given it the time. He had helped on the school, but he couldn't ring them in. He had topped Saint Philip's steeple, but it wasn't the top. The top was a golden vane, a weather cock. Cock, clock, bell and at the chapel a spike to draw lightning. Wind, time, voice and fire – they were all the smith!

Joseph's palm sweated on the cold iron latch of the big school door. Inside the hall he heard the end of prayers.

The carpenter couldn't lock the door. The carpenter could never open it or close. Latch, lock, hinges were the smith.

Joseph looked down. The step was stone, and he would not cross it for his last day. Still holding, he faced about.

The school porch showed the view, a stone arch around the world, and Grandfather had made that. It framed Saint Philip's steeple and the weathercock.

And then Joseph knew.

That great steeple, that great work. It was a pattern left on sand and air. The glint of the sun from the weathercock shimmered his gaze, and the gleam was about the stone right to the earth. He saw golden brushes, the track of combing chisels, every mark. The stone was only the finish of the blow. The church was the print of chisels in the sky.

Joseph let go of the latch handle. Behind him was the step into the hall. In front of him was the step through the arch. Not even for his last day could he go to school. There was no time. He stood between stone and stone.

"No back bargains!" shouted Joseph, and did a standing leap through the arch. He fell over and rolled on the ground.

Joseph breathed in. The weathercock raced the clouds.

He walked away from the school, past the church, over the station bridge, towards the chapel clock. Nothing he saw or could think of went beyond the smith. Shoes on the horses, their bridles and brasses, the iron of the coach wheels, the planes, blades, adzes, axes, bradawls and bits led to the forge. Even the hands on the clock. Without that fire there was no time.

Joseph went into the farrier's yard and down to the cellar. The apprentice was working the bellows handle: up and down, and up and down. The cellar breathed.

Joseph stood quietly, just looking.

"What are you after, youth?"

The smith was behind him, at the top of the steps in the yard.

"Will you set me on?" said Joseph. "I'll be prenticed to you."

"Shall you?" said the smith. "Come up, then."

He was a big man, in his shirt sleeves; a leather brat, tied round his waist, reached below his knees. He bent and put his arms under the farrier's anvil, lifted it from its bed, carried it across the yard and set it down.

"Now take it back," he said to Joseph.

Joseph put his arms around the anvil and lifted. His chin jarred on the top. He tried again, firming his chin against the steel. Nothing moved. But it was not like stone; not like the rough dead weight that tore on Damper Latham's planks.

"I can't shift it," said Joseph.

"A smith carries his anvil."

"Well I can't yet."

"You can't shift an anvil," said the smith, "yet you want to join the generous, ingenious hammermen? You can't shift an anvil, but you want your own sledge?"

"I do," said Joseph.

"Then give me one reason why I should set you on," said the smith. "Why should I take me another prentice for six years of no gain? You're old Robert's lad, aren't you?"

"Ay."

"The granny reardun?"

"But me mother's coming up our house for her dinner."

"You're still a granny reardun."

Joseph said nothing.

"And what does Robert think?"

"I've not told him," said Joseph.

"Not told him? You're a previous sort of a youth, aren't you?"

"I've not had chance," said Joseph.

"Then you'd best make chance," said the smith. "And I'm still waiting to hear why I should put meself out to find sufficient meat, drink, apparel, washing and lodging for a prentice as can't shift his anvil."

"Because a smith's aback of everything," said Joseph.

"He's what did you say?"

"Aback of everything. He's master."

The smith went to a chest of drawers in the yard, opened the top drawer and took out a roll of parchment paper.

"Can you tell me what this is?" he said.

"It's called an Indenture," said Joseph.

"And an Indenture is a legal document," said the smith.

"I know," said Joseph.

"Binding you and me."

Joseph nodded.

"Can you read?" said the smith.

"Ay," said Joseph.

"Write?"

"Ay."

"Well, I'm beggared if I can," said the smith. "Anyroad: a prentice, it says here, is to be learned the art, craft and mystery of the forge."

Joseph felt as if everything around him had stopped but those words.

"And he shall faithfully serve the hammerman, his secrets keep, his lawful commands everywhere gladly obey."

Joseph put his hands between his knees, and listened.

"At cards, dice or any unlawful game he shall not play. He shall not absent himself, day or night, nor haunt ale houses, taverns or playhouses, commit fornication nor contract for matrimony."

"I'll not," said Joseph.

"You'll be a rum un if you don't," said the smith. "But that's it. That's what it says."

"I'll go tell me Grandfather now," said Joseph.

"When can you start?" said the smith.

"As soon as I've shifted this anvil," said Joseph.

"Wait on, now!" The smith laughed. "Robert and me must have us a proper weisening about you first." He picked up the anvil and firmed it back on its bed. "And that," he said, "you'll lift just before you're out of your time, because by then, youth, we'll have put some muscle on you. Now get off up home and tell your Grandfather. And take this four-pounder Damper Latham asked for."

He gave Joseph a steel hammer-head, blunt at one end, and sharp for splitting at the other, with a hole through it for its haft.

Joseph held it up. "See," he said. "It is aback of everything."

"Tell that to Robert!" said the smith. "And think on: you can play wag from school, but you'll not play wag from me."

Joseph walked below the chapel clock. He could hear its tick.

When he reached the wood he climbed up the slope among the beech trees, so that Grandfather wouldn't see him. He wanted to choose his moment. There was a lot of distant noise coming off Leah's Bank.

The road was empty. Grandfather was not at the wall, nor was he anywhere that Joseph could tell from the wood.

Joseph strode, slack-kneed, down through the leaf-mould of the hill. It was the way to move, even at night, so that roots and rocks wouldn't catch the feet and he kept the rhythm of the ground.

Grandfather's bass was tucked behind the field hedge. All his tools were there. Joseph put the new hammer-head with them.

"Where is he?" he said.

There was another load of stone dumped at the end of the run of wall, but it wasn't rubbish: it was square-cut white dimension, weathered, good. A barrow-load only.

"Grandfather!"

Some of the stone was white with lime-wash on one side. Joseph touched it. The lime was still wet.

"Grandfather!"

"Who-whoop!"

It was Grandfather's shout. It carried a mile on the hill, and Grandmother always used it to call him home.

"Wo-whoop! Wo-o-o-o!" answered Joseph.

"Who-whoop!" cried Grandfather some-where.

"Wo-whoop! Wo-o-o-o!"

"Who-whoop!"

Grandfather was coming from the house. He appeared over the road crest a hundred yards away. He walked strongly.

" 'Therefore, behold, I will hedge up thy way with thorns, and make a wall!' "

Grandfather knew the Bible whenever he was drunk.

" 'And I will destroy her vines and her fig trees! And I will make them a forest! And the beasts of the field shall eat them!' "

His eyes were bright and his face was a good colour. That was all. He stood and inspected the work he had done, and he lifted his cap and rubbed his forehead with the knuckle of his thumb.

"What a wall," said Grandfather. "Looks like it died in a fog."

Then he was splendid.

He took the new stone, the square dimension, and he built. He smoothed and combed the blocks, and they fitted together with hardly a knife-space between them. Their weight was nothing for him, and Joseph watched the old man happy.

The wall was being built. No limewash showed, no donkey-stoning. "There," said Grandfather.

"Why?" shouted Joseph. "Why've you taken it? Why you?"

"That's a poser," said Grandfather. "Eh up. Here's a new four-pounder in me little bass."

"Why?"

"You fetched it, I reckon. Or Damper Latham."

"The stone! Allmans' stone!"

"So it is," said Grandfather. "Ay. Young Herbert wheeled me a barrow-load. I could do with another."

"I'll not!" shouted Joseph, and ran.

He ran all the way home, up the garden path, through the doorway, up the bent stairs and fell on his bed under the limewash and the sloping thatch. He lay there, grasping the corner post of the house to hold the world. The lime flaked off the oak. It needed a new coat. And all the time there was the noise on Leah's Bank, a swearing, tearing noise, and dust from it finely settled his tears.

Joseph heard Mother come, and Charlie. The bassinet grated on the path. Charlie wanted his dinner, but Joseph couldn't go down to see him. There was that noise.

Grandmother and Mother went into the back garden to pick peas. Joseph waited until the inside of the downstairs was quiet, then he crept out.

Charlie was parked under the thatch away from the sun. He laughed at Joseph, and Joseph played with him. The bassinet was lop-sided because a spring had broken. Mother had brought it for Grandfather to mend.

Joseph helped shell the peas, and he gave the little ones to Charlie. Mother peeled the potatoes. It was going to be a big dinner.

"Have you played wag?" said Grandfather.

Joseph didn't answer.

"Well, you can go help Damper Latham this after," said Grandfather. "I've a flavour for to finish that wall."

"Where?" said Joseph.

"Long Croft, you pan-head."

"Where with Damper Latham?"

"Leah's Bank. Where else?"

"I'll not."

"And I'll catch you a clinker if I hear any more of that," said Grandfather. "Where's me dinner?" he shouted, and poured himself more beer.

Joseph fed Charlie, and played with him again. Grandfather fitted the haft to the new hammer-head and dropped it in the rain-butt to swell. Then he tied the bassinet together with rope.

"Put that Charlie of yours down," Grandfather said to Joseph. "Play wag at end of schooling, and you're half a day a man's lad. Let's be having you."

They went down the path together. The noise on the hill was no better.

"You get yourself up them fields and tell Damper Latham I've sent you. I'll ready the bank."

"Just why?" said Joseph.

Grandfather looked at him before he spoke. And when he did speak he was not drunk. There was no beer in him talking.

"Why," he said. "Why. Must I cut me nose off to spite me face?"

"But Allmans," said Joseph.

"Is it me making that racket yonder?" said Grandfather. "It is not. They've got allsorts there – men as couldn't tell foxbench from malachite. So what must I do? Let it go? Let it all go? For a garden? Or shall I have a word with the Governor, and slip him a sixpence? Eh? That garden wall will never be nothing. But all your days you'll pass the dimension by Long Croft, and you'll say, 'Ay, he was a bazzil-arsed old devil, but him and me, we built that!' "

And Joseph couldn't tell him.

They went to their work.

The house was terrible on Leah's Bank. Its roof and the gable ends were off. The stone slates had been sent down and stacked by size, Princesses, Duchesses, Small Count-

esses, Ladies, Wide Doubles and the neat Jenny-go-lightlies from under the ridge. The sheepbone pegs that had held them to the roof were scattered on the ground, as if the house was eaten.

Timbers had been sorted; common rafters, purlins, joists, trusses, wind-braces and bearers.

And Young Herbert Allman was daylabouring for the men.

The house was down to its eaves. Only the bedroom window stood higher, showing sky from both sides through its glass.

Young Herbert stopped his barrowing. He said nothing. He picked up Mrs Allman's donkey-stone from beside the dirtied step, lifted his arm and winged the donkeystone straight to the pane. Then he still said nothing, and got on with his load.

Joseph took a lump of rubble from the wall-packing and watched the window. The broken pane was clean now.

He let go. The rock lobbed over and over and hit. The window burst with a sound

44

that Joseph felt in his stomach. It was so good he did it again.

"And is that what a man's lad thinks of his first half-day?" said Damper Latham.

He was walking round the building to put his chalk mark on likely stone.

"Has Robert sent you?"

"He has," said Joseph.

"To chuck cob-ends at windows? You're a constructive sort of a youth, aren't you?"

"It's . . . them!" said Joseph.

"It's not," said Damper Latham. "It's you."

"I've not ridded Allmans! I've not wrecked this!"

"Give over gondering at what can't be helped," said Damper Latham.

Joseph pulled aside the stones that Damper Latham had marked. The noise around him was no less, and through it Young Herbert barrowed.

The stone was as heavy as before. Joseph's hands blistered.

Yet the anvil was heavier than stone, and the forge louder than the hill. But he wanted them. He wanted metals that could be made and the sounds of making. He could not forget the limewashed walls of the morning. For this.

"Tea up!" shouted the Governor. The men stopped, and squatted on the grass. Damper Latham gave Joseph a drink from his bottle. The sweetness calmed him. The hill was quiet. He knew where he was once more on Leah's Bank above his own house.

The sun caught movement at Long Croft field, reflection on a chisel, and the sound of Grandfather's hammer could just be heard, like a small bell.

Even the ruin was gentle now. It had its place.

"It was me," Joseph said to Damper Latham. "I was that upset."

"Ay."

"What's to become of it all?" said Joseph.

"Oh, not much," said Damper Latham. "They'll have the house down in the day. Then it'll go to nettles, a ruck of stones, and cussing every time Jesse Leah catches his scythe on a bit of a doorstep. But at after, and before you know, there'll be only meadow and a hump to it by a gate, and some damson tresses in a hedge without sense nor reason. And that's all. Now hadn't you ought go and tell him?"

"Who?"

"Your Grandfather."

"Tell him what?"

"About old Jump setting you on."

Joseph startled, and couldn't speak.

"You're gondering again, youth," said Damper Latham. "Well, is he or isn't he?"

"How did you hear?" said Joseph.

"Hear? Jump and me's had us eye on you this twelvemonth and more. It's in you."

"What is?"

"Smithing, of course!"

"In me," said Joseph.

"And it'll out, one road or the other," said Damper Latham. "Hinder, and you'll turn sour as verjuice."

"Does me Grandfather know?" said Joseph.

47

"There's not but one can face Robert with that news," said Damper Latham.

"Me?" said Joseph. Leah's Bank was hushed. Men went back to work, but the noise no longer hurt. Pick-axes, pinch-bars, crows, wedges, sledges battered and prized the house. Dust shimmered Joseph's gaze in the sun, and out of it he could remember before breakfast, and now see the track of picks, with stone the finish of the blow, and not all smithing was making.

"Me," said Joseph. "Me."

"I'll be along with the dimension in half an hour," said Damper Latham.

"I'll tell him I'll tell him I'll tell him!" shouted Joseph, and ran down Leah's Bank.

"I'll tell him I'll tell him I'll tell him. I'll tell him I'll tell him I'll tell him. I'll tell him. I'll tell him. Tell him. I'll tell him."

"Eh up!" Grandfather called. "You! Charge of the Light Brigade! Balaclava's that road!"

Joseph stopped, breathless.

"Ay," said Grandfather. "I recollect as

how they lost their puff a bit, too. I was cutting bell-cot for the school at the time."

"Grandfather," said Joseph. He was leaning against the rock of the hill, in the shade of beeches. "I'll not go with you."

"What?" said Grandfather.

Joseph stood straight. "I'll not cut stone."

"You'll not what?" said Grandfather.

"I can't. You must prentice me to the smithy."

Grandfather laid his tools down.

"Prentice to the smithy? Prentice to little Jump James?"

"That's what you must do," said Joseph. "I've to get me Indentures. I don't want stone."

"You don't want stone," said Grandfather.

"No."

"And why don't you want stone?"

"Because," said Joseph.

"Because?" said Grandfather. "Because of what?"

The words blurted out. "Because of you!"

"Oh." Grandfather was still.

"You're all over!" said Joseph. "I must get somewhere: somewhere aback of you. I must. It's my time. Else I'll never."

Grandfather took off his cap and threw it on the road.

"By God!"

He stamped on his cap, and turned around.

"By God!" He stamped again. "Joseph, I thought you'd never speak!"

"Eh?" said Joseph.

"Smithing! By God, that's aback, that is! That's aback of behind!"

"You're not vexed?"

"Vexed? Me?" said Grandfather. "Who'll make the brick-setter's trowel, Joseph? Who'll make the brickie's trowel? Hey!"

His beard danced and he held Joseph at arm's length. "Who-whoop! Wo-whoop! Wo-o-o-o! Who'll make the brickie's trowel? Wo-whoop! Wo-o-o-o!"

Damper Latham came over the crest at

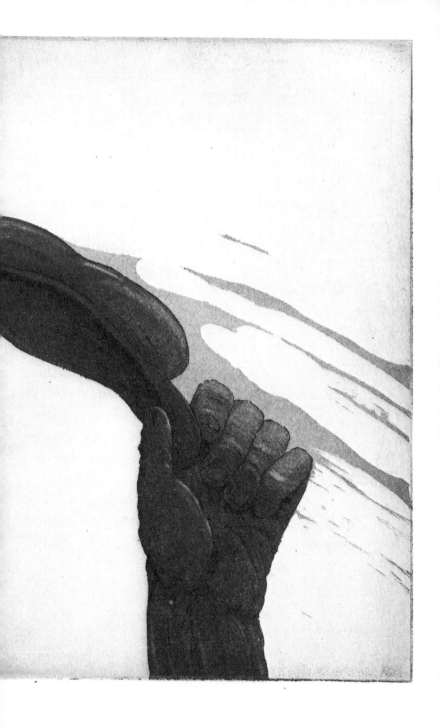

the top of Long Croft field.

Grandfather pulled Joseph with him to the bank. "Act natural," he said. "Give us a thrutch with this." He was lifting a stone into its seat. Joseph eased the ends, and Grandfather tapped the stone sideways with the handle of his hammer. He could have managed it by himself, without help. "There," he said. "She'll do. You'll be able to say we built that one."

"Never think I'm against you," said Joseph. "I've got to carry me own sledge at the forge."

"And you shall," said Grandfather. "Stone and you, you'd never marry: I've seen it, Joseph. And, Joseph, we do us best, but you're a granny reardun, think on, and a granny reardun you'll be. So you get prenticed, and a roof over you, and meat in you, and drink. You're like to have to look to yourself sooner than most in this world. Hey!" he shouted to Damper Latham. "My grandson! See at him! He's going for a generous, ingenious hammerman!"

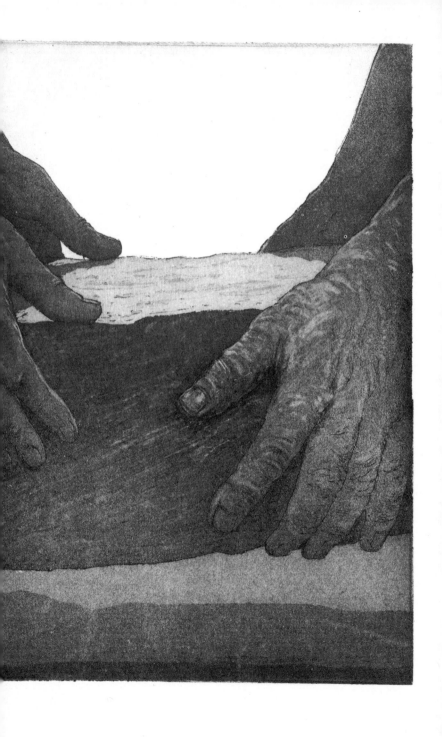

"He's never!" said Damper Latham. "Woa back!" he said to the horses.

"He is that! Prenticed to little Jump James! What do you think?"

"His Indentures'll need some wetting," said Damper Latham. "Shall I be invited?"

"I'll go see Jump tonight," said Grandfather. "Then it'll be all round the anvil tomorrow and a new barrel from The Bull's Head. Now what've you fetched me?" He looked into the cart. "Gorgeous," he said. "Beautiful. Oh, that's the ticket for soup! Let's be having it."

He unfastened the sides. Joseph tried to help him, but Grandfather wouldn't let him.

"No," he said. "Not my grandson. I'm not having his touch spoilt with raunging."

Damper winked. "Give us a tune, youth," he said, and passed the E-Flat cornet to Joseph.

"You'd best keep her," he said. "She's a good un, but she's an old un, and she'll need looking after now and again to keep her sweet. What do you say, Robert?"

54

"Oh, he's the only best tinsmith already," said Grandfather. "He'll be learning Jump a thing or two."

Joseph held the cornet, the brass metal.

"You mean it?" he said to Damper Latham.

Damper Latham winked, but differently. There was a sparkle, and he just waved his hand.

Joseph went to the wood and sat in a beech tree root. Grandfather and Damper Latham began to unload the white dimension stone. Joseph sat above them, and played.

The men banged the stones off, and sang.

"Oh, can you wash a soldier's shirt?
And can you wash it clean?
Oh, can you wash a soldier's shirt,
And hang it on the green?"

Joseph played it over and over, faster and faster, descants and triple-tonguing. It was the great song of the Hough, and it never tired.

Damper Latham clapped his cart to, and drove off, beating time still with his curled whip, in the air.

Joseph strode down the wood, loose-legged, and playing, and jigged on the road. He stopped only to polish the shining cornet on the edge of his sleeve; his own cornet, soprano E-Flat.

"Oh, can you wash a soldier's shirt?
And can you wash it clean?
Oh, can you wash a soldier's shirt . . ."

He heard the crake, crake of the broken spring on the bassinet. Mother was coming down the slope of the road by Long Croft field, taking Charlie home for his tea.

". . . And hang it on the green?"

Joseph ran. "See at it! See at it!" he cried. "See at it! Me own! And I'm to be a prenticed smith!"

He always pushed Charlie down Long Croft and under the wood. Charlie liked the speed and rattle of it and the wind in the holes in the bassinet hood.

Joseph set off, full belt, one-handed, playing the cornet with the other. The spring that Grandfather could hold only with rope made the wheels veer to the left. Joseph and Charlie swerved down the hill.

> *"Oh, can you wash a soldier's shirt?*
> *And can you wash it clean?*
> *Oh, can you wash a soldier's shirt,*
> *And hang it on the green?"*

Grandfather took off his cap and whirled it around his head as they passed.

"Who-whoop! Wo-whoop! Wo-o-o-o!"

"Who-whoop! Wo-whoop! Wo-o-o-o!" Joseph answered. The roped spring grated and bounced. Joseph ran on.

"Never mind, Charlie. Wait while I get me sledge. You'll see! I'll mend your bassinet!"

"Who-whoop! Wo-whoop! Wo-o-o-o!"

Charlie laughed. Under the earth, the forge bloomed. Cornet and weathercock, the sun shone, music, turning to the wind.